OUR MICHIGAN!

We Love the Seasons

Illustrated by GIJSBERT VAN FRANKENHUYZEN

PUBLISHED BY SLEEPING BEAR PRESS

Spring
in
MICHIGAN
is . . .

Walking near a pond and listening to the frogs croaking. Who is that standing near the water?

Playing tag in a birch glen. Are fairies hiding among the trees?

Running through meadows,
picking flowers for daisy chains.
Let's see who is fastest!

Summer

in

MICHIGAN

is . . .

Curling our toes in the sand
as waves roar in. Let's collect
pretty rocks and shells.

Riding the ferryboat as it bobs up and down in the bright blue waves. Can you hear the gull caw?

Counting the stars in the sky
as the lighthouse beams its light.
Star light, star bright . . . Who
saw the first star tonight?

Autumn in MICHIGAN is . . .

Hiking in fields as birds fly through the sky. How many can you count?

Racing through golden woods, hearing dry leaves scrunch underfoot.
Snap! Crackle! Pop!

Daydreaming as the sun sets
over green-gold hills. Let's write
a poem to celebrate the day.

Winter *in* MICHIGAN *is . . .*

Smelling the smoke from a wood fire on a snowy afternoon. Look— the trees have lost their leaves.

Crunching through snow during a walk in the moonlight. Let's look for pine cones near the trees. *Who-oo* is that hiding up in the tree?

Staying up late to watch lights
dance across the night sky.
Count the rainbow colors!

Let's start the year over
and do it all again!

Nature Craft Activities

There is no better way to celebrate special times outdoors than using "outdoor supplies" that you can collect during nature walks. The best part is that everything is free. The most important thing to remember when gathering outdoor materials is to be a responsible collector.

A responsible collector remembers to do the following:

- Look for dead or fallen materials first. Pine needles, dried leaves, empty shells, and rocks are not alive. You are not disturbing nature too much if you remove only small amounts of these materials.

- Check with an adult *before* picking anything from a living plant. You don't want to pick something poisonous, such as poison ivy or sumac, by mistake. Also, you need to be sure you are not picking a plant that may be endangered.

- Never take materials from someone else's property without asking.

- Watch out for animals. The outdoors is their home! You should never disturb a wasps' nest. Don't take eggs out of a bird's nest. And never cover the hole of an underground burrow.

- Disturb nature as little as possible. Try to leave an area as you found it.

Be sure to ask an adult for help with these craft activities if you need it.
Have fun creating these crafts to celebrate your nature walks!

How to Make a Flower Chain

Materials you will need:
Daisies

Selecting your daisies

- Look for daisies with thick stems that are at least 4 inches (10 centimeters) long. Look for healthy, fully open flowers for a more beautiful chain.

1. With your thumbnail, cut a small slit through the middle of the stem without breaking it in half. You can make your cut just below the flower or halfway down the stem. If your nail is too short, use a plastic knife (under adult supervision).

2. Thread the stem of another daisy through the slit. Push the base of the stem through until the flower is snug against the slit.

3. Repeat with any number of daisies. Make a slit in the next daisy and push the third stem through it. Repeat until you've made a bracelet, crown, or necklace.

4. When you think your daisy chain is long enough, cut a second slit through the first stem. Push the last daisy through this slit to make a loop.

Keep for yourself or share with a friend!

 # How to Press Fall Leaves

Materials you will need:
Leaves
Scissors
Clear contact paper

Selecting your leaves

- Select leaves that are relatively flat and not curling around the edges.

- Look for leaves that do not have spots or bumps.

- You can use leaves in various stages of changing colors.

- The drier the leaf, the better it will press.

1. Sort your leaves on a large tabletop or other flat surface.

2. Cut two pieces of contact paper to the size you want. Set one piece aside. From the first piece, remove the contact paper and place it sticky side UP on the table.

3. Arrange your leaves on the sticky paper in any pattern or shape you choose.

4. Remove the contact paper from your second piece and place it sticky side DOWN on top of your leaves. Press firmly around each leaf and across the entire sheet of paper.

You can keep this project intact as a set of colorful leaves to hang on a wall or refrigerator, or you can cut them out individually and share with friends!

For more outdoor craft activities, please visit
https://sleepingbearpress.com/teaching_guides.

Mr. van Frankenhuyzen thanks the Woodlands of DeWitt for the loan of two of his paintings from their collection.

SLEEPING BEAR PRESS™

2395 South Huron Parkway, Suite 200
Ann Arbor, MI 48104
www.sleepingbearpress.com

Printed and bound in the United States.

10 9 8 7 6 5 4 3 2 1

Library of Congress Cataloging-in-Publication Data

Names: Frankenhuyzen, Gijsbert van, illustrator.
Title: Our Michigan! we love the seasons / illustrated by Gijsbert van Frankenhuyzen.
Description: Ann Arbor, MI : Sleeping Bear Press, [2021] | Audience: Ages 4-8. |
Summary: Easy-to-read text and illustrations of nature scenes in Michigan celebrate
what makes each season of the year special. Includes nature craft activities.
Identifiers: LCCN 2020038593 | ISBN 9781534111356 (hardcover)
Subjects: LCSH: Michigan--Juvenile fiction. | CYAC: Michigan—Fiction. | Seasons—Fiction.
Classification: LCC PZ7.1.F7516 Our 2021 | DDC [E]—dc23
LC record available at https://lccn.loc.gov/2020038593